TAKEN BY THE TIGER KING

KENZIE SKYE

CHAPTER
ONE

Raoul

I prowl along the city streets, my senses on high alert—as ever. I know what I'm looking for, but I don't know how I'll know when I find it. All I know is that I will *know*. And I know that doesn't make much sense, but that's the way of our mating.

To the disappointment of many of the females in our streak, none of them call to me as my mate, and tiger streaks aren't the same as lion prides. Whereas if a lion doesn't find his fated mate in his pride, he will still marry within his pride, settling for less just to keep the bloodline pure, that's not the way of us tigers. We know that not only will marrying your true fated mate make you as strong as you can be, but it will lead to a happier tiger who will perform better for the entire streak. It not only benefits the tiger in question, but the streak as a whole, and since I am the tiger king, it's doubly important for me to find my fated mate rather than settling. I'm not only seeking her for my own happiness, but for the well-being of my entire streak.

Still, it's a bitch and a pain in my ass that I couldn't have been fated to one of the females in my streak. It certainly would have made this a lot easier. But, of course, as fate would have it, I have yet to stumble across my mate, so I'm out here looking for her.

It's unlikely I'll find her at work since most of the businesses my streak runs are employed almost exclusively by members of our streak. The lions might have their hands in oil and all the transportation businesses, but us tigers are in control of most of the agricultural ones. I happen to be the CEO of the biggest agricultural importing and exporting business in the city.

I snarl when I walk past the lion king's high rise. The fuckers keep charging so much for gas prices, and it's making it more difficult for my business to turn a profit. It's also making it difficult for the entire population because everybody needs food, and that's what my business supplies.

The fucking lions are the supposed kings of the jungle. They're supposed to look out for everyone, but they're nothing but a bunch of cutthroats looking to gouge anyone any way they can. They essentially fuck the entire world up the ass.

I continue to walk along the street amongst all the humans and other shifters going about their day-to-day work. Of course, the humans know about us shifters. They know the lions are in charge of the oil and the tigers are in charge of agriculture and that the wolves just don't give a fuck and like to stay off in the mountains to themselves. Wolves have always been selfish creatures. The bears are over the fishing industry and help the humans somewhat.

Regardless, there's one thing all of us shifters have in common. We have designated reservations where we do our shifting. When we're around humans and within city limits, we're to remain in our human form at all times. That is the one big law among our kind concerning the humans. While the humans know there are shifters among them, they can't tell just by looking at us what we are, and it just stresses so many of them to see one of us shift in front of them. Plus, it's also detrimental to their safety oftentimes, so that's why the council over the shifters put the law in place in the first place. It's much more difficult to control our animalistic natures when we're in our animal forms, and that oftentimes leads to humans getting hurt. They're such delicate creatures, sensitive and in need of our care and protection, whether or not they realize it.

I scowl, my irritation rising to new heights as I realize my search has been fruitless. It could take me years to find my mate at this rate, and I'm impatient enough as it is. I can't focus on properly ruling my streak with this insatiable need inside me. I'm a tiger in his prime, and my biological clock is screaming at me to take my mate. And I would gladly do so if only I could find her.

I grunt as someone bumps into me—hard. But the impact doesn't hurt me at all or barely budge me. Still, it's enough to garner my attention, and my hands shoot out to steady the tiny female in front of me before she topples to the ground. A reprimand about how she should watch where she's going is on the tip of my tongue. I'm usually not so rude, but she caught me in a bad moment.

My sharp words die on my tongue, though, when her eyelashes flutter up to me. I'm assaulted by her big blue eyes. They're a crystal-clear blue, the blue of a cloudless sky on a summer day. My chest tightens as they hold me captive. I'm unable to tear my gaze from their shining depths.

My breathing becomes ragged as all the neurons in my brain fire. My blood rushes through my veins, hot and heavy. I'm hyper-aware of her bare shoulders underneath my fingertips where I'm still gripping her. The feeling of her skin underneath mine sends electricity shooting through my palms and up my arms.

Her puffy pink lips fall open in a little gasp, and I finally tear my eyes away from her blue orbs long enough to note that her hair is a fiery red. It's a beautiful mane of curls that cascades down her back in luxurious waves. She looks like one of those pretty porcelain dolls women collect. Her skin is creamy and silky and smooth. I can tell she's not wearing any makeup, yet she's flawless. She looks too flawless to be real.

She smells young and innocent and ripe, like fresh berries. She's undoubtedly a virgin and young. So very young. Dainty. Pretty. Gorgeous. There aren't enough adjectives to describe what she is, what she makes me feel.

I already know she's my mate before a word comes out of her mouth, so all the other points are moot. Still, I ask her anyway, "How old are you?"

Her pretty brow furrows, and she looks up at me in confusion. "What?" Her voice is so soft and pretty, like a light tinkling of bells, and fuck if it doesn't make my cock hard.

"Are you eighteen?" I ask her, my voice coming out more roughly than I intend.

She blinks at me obviously, taken aback before she bristles. "No."

My heart plummets. Fuck, how can she be my mate if she's not even of legal age...

"I'm nineteen."

Relief crashes through me. Humans claim to understand a bit of our mating rituals, but they have their own laws. I don't need to be making trouble with them by getting involved with a minor, so thank fuck, my mate is legal. She's barely legal, but legal.

I inhale a deep breath, trying to get a deeper read on her scent. I don't smell any shifter in her at all. She's pure human, and while it's not unheard of for shifters to have a human mate, it's rare for someone higher in the hierarchy like me. A tiger king almost always has a shifter mate, someone who understands the streak's ways and can help him with his leadership.

My little mate is certainly no tigress, but there's no helping it. Every atom in my body is screaming at me she's the one, and I'm helpless to fight this even if I wanted to. Which I don't.

My eyes greedily drink her in. My mate is beautiful. She's everything I could have ever wanted and more. I never imagined one so perfect. The way I'm staring at her must start to freak her out because she pulls against my hold and apologizes weakly, "Yeah, I'm sorry I bumped into you. I'm late for work—"

She lets out a little oomph as I suddenly pick her up and fling her over my shoulder caveman style. I don't give a fuck that we're in the middle of a busy street. I dare anyone to try to stop me from taking my mate.

She screeches, "Put me down!" She tries to kick, but I band my arm around her legs and hold her little dress down so that no other males get a flash of the sweet ass that is mine. The scent of her pussy drifts over to my nostrils, and I inhale deeply, precum leaking from the tip of my cock in response.

I begin stalking down the street with her. A few humans stop and stare, but none dare challenge me. I can tell who the shifters are already because one glance at us and they look hurriedly away, knowing better than to get involved in the tiger king's claiming of his mate. They know very well what's going on.

My mate keeps kicking and screaming as I carry her into my building and go straight for the elevator. Only when we're locked inside do I set her on her feet and stare down at her intently, taking in the beautiful flush to her cheeks and the way her blue eyes are flashing with anger rather than fear.

"What's your name?" I demand, needing to know what to call my mate. I can't keep referring to her as "mate." That, and I'm genuinely interested in knowing what my mate's name is. I want to know everything about her.

Instead of answering me, she soundly slaps me across the cheek.

I grin as I feel the sting.

Oh yes, she will make a fine tiger queen.

TWO

Mya

I expect the big, hulking man to be pissed that I've just slapped him. I've never struck anyone in my entire life, and if I had any good sense, I would be trembling with fear after having the audacity to hit this man who is more than twice my size. Seriously, he would put the Hulk to shame with his bulging muscles and tall stature.

Only he's not a big green giant. He's more like a beautiful, sandy-haired Herculean god. His hair is a beautiful golden brown that flows down to his shoulders. Swear to god, he looks like one of those men from the cover of Highlander romance novels.

It looks like it's all his shirt can do to contain the bulk of his muscles, and his thighs are like cannons. He has a square jaw line with stubble already lining it this early in the day, like he has so much testosterone it immediately sprouts soon as he shaves.

The man is every woman's dream, but that doesn't give him the right to fling me over his shoulder like I'm nothing more than a sack of potatoes and stomp off with me as if he has any right. Just because he's handsome doesn't mean he can't be a psycho or a serial killer.

Instead of looking angry, though, the man's eyes flare with heat, and a grin pulls at the corners of his mouth. Okay, so maybe he's not a serial killer, but he's definitely still a psycho. He has to be insane to *enjoy* the slap I delivered him. My palm is still stinging from it.

And that pisses me off because I suspect that the slap literally hurt me more than it hurt him. "What's your name, hellcat?" He's looking down at me with his handsome face, and I feel a growl tearing up my throat at the nickname.

"Shouldn't you ask someone that before you kidnap them?" I hiss at him.

He just smiles at me now. It's a breathtakingly handsome smile of full, white, even teeth. "I'm Raoul Cunnings," he offers his own name, no doubt hoping to coax mine from me by this gesture.

I cross my arms over my chest and glare at him icily as the elevator continues to take us up, up, up. Jesus, how far up are we going?

"Well, look, mister—" I begin, but the hulking man in front of me interrupts me.

"Raoul," he corrects me.

"Raoul." I grit my teeth as I say his name. "I'm really sorry I bumped into you, but don't you think this is a little over the top?" I laugh nervously. "Are you going to kill me for just trying to get to work on time?" I glanced down at the watch on my wrist, my stomach dropping when I see that I'm later than ever know. "Shit, my boss is going to kill me," I groan.

"No, he won't," Raoul tells me reassuringly.

I raised my brows at him and scoff. "So, you're not only a kidnapper, you're a stalker too? Do you happen to know who my boss is?"

He gives a nonchalant shrug. "No, but it

doesn't matter because you don't work there anymore."

I gawk at him. "What?"

"If you want to work, you can work for me now, but you don't have to work if you don't want to."

I stare at the man like he's just sprouted two heads. Okay, this guy is certifiably insane. What is he even talking about?

He suddenly yanks my purse from my shoulder and starts digging through it. "Hey!" I protest, mortified. "You can't just go through a woman's purse!"

He doesn't answer me. Instead, he finally finds what he's looking for and pulls out my wallet. He flips it open, and when his eyes flick back up to me, there's triumph in them. "How else was I going to find out your name, stubborn little Mya?"

That's all he wanted? To find out my name? Not to rob me or something? But that thought is ridiculous anyway. Why would this man want to rob me? I'm scraping by to make ends meet, and his clothing looks expensive. Everything about the man screams rich and powerful.

This whole interaction with this man has been bizarre, and I internally curse myself for ever having the misfortune to bump into him. The elevator finally dings and then opens. Raoul takes my hand and pulls me out onto what looks to be the top floor of the tallest high rise in the city.

I gasp at the view that's presented to me through the floor-to-ceiling windows. It looks like we're at the very top of the city.

Who the hell is this guy that he has a view like this? I glance around and notice that we're in what looks to be an opulent office. There's a desk set up, but then the rest of the space looks like a luxurious penthouse suite. There's a couch and television and fireplace and all the modern luxuries you would find in any an expensive city apartment. Still, this doesn't make any sense.

"What's going on?" I ask him in confusion. "Why did you bring me here? What do you want with me?"

Raoul stalks slowly over to me, his nostrils flared and his chest heaving up and down. His eyes are pinned on me like a predator stalking its prey, and I feel a shiver go up my spine, though I'm not entirely sure whether it's a shiver of fear or something else.

"Everything, Mya. I want *everything*." The look in his eyes is so intense. I instinctively begin backing up. With every step he takes toward me, I take one away from him until my back hits the wall.

My heart hammers in my chest, but he keeps drawing closer and closer. All I wanted was to get to work on time and now I find myself in the most bizarre situation of my entire life. Can a girl ever catch a break?

Raoul

It's probably fucked up that I'm getting turned on by her retreating from me, but it calls to the natural predator in me. I can't help skating my eyes over her from head to toe. Everything about her calls to me. Every cell in my body is screaming at me to claim her. She's my mate, and I want nothing more than to shove my cock deep inside her and impregnate her so I can tie her to me forever.

Judging by the way she swallows hard when I tell her I want everything from her, she's not going to fall right into my arms. It's going to take some wooing to get my little mate to agree to bed me because despite how much my instincts are screaming at me to claim her, I'm no rapist. When I finally claim her as my own, it will be with her consent.

That doesn't mean I can't mark my little Mya, though.

Mya.

Just the thought of her name sends fire licking through my veins. It's so perfect. Just like her. It's the only name I care about now.

Mya. My mate. Mine.

I finally back her up against the wall and clap my hands against the wall on either side of her, effectively caging her in under my body.

I love seeing her like this, eyes wide, lips slightly parted, those red curls wild around her face and shoulders, captured by me.

I can't resist and press my body fully against her, letting her feel the hardness of my cock pressing into her soft stomach.

She gasps and tries to wiggle away from me, but there's nowhere for her to go. I moan at the friction she's creating against my throbbing length.

"If you don't want to lose your virginity right

here and now, you'll stop wiggling on my cock like that, hellcat."

Her eyes widen even more as she sputters, "How did—how did you know I was a virgin?"

"I can smell it on you," I growl as I inhale a deep breath of her sweet, innocent, virgin scent.

Her brow furrows adorably until her eyes widen with comprehension. She looks up at me with new horror. "Oh my god. You're a shifter?"

I frown down at her. "You say that like I'm a serial killer."

She shakes her head as she begins to plead. "Please, this is all a mistake. Just let me go."

I don't know what she's so afraid of, but I try to set her fears at ease. "I'll never harm you, little hellcat. You have nothing to be afraid of with me."

She shakes her head again as if she can't believe the situation she's gotten herself in. She doesn't realize there was nothing she could have done to avoid this. It's fate. She's my mate, so the universe was bound to bring us together at some point or another.

"Why have you taken me?" she asks me again.

"Because you're my mate," I tell her simply, my voice heated with lust at saying the words out loud.

She makes a strangled sound and begins fighting for freedom, kicking and punching against me as she tries to break the stronghold of my arms. She's hissing and snarling, and I can't help thinking I nicknamed her appropriately. She is indeed a little hellcat. My little hellcat.

While it stings my ego to see her reaction at the thought of being mated to me, I try to remind myself that humans are complicated creatures. She needs time to adjust, and that's fine. I'll give it to her, but I'm not letting her go. Not now that I've finally found her.

"Stop, Mya." My voice cracks through the air like a whip. Every tiger in my pride stands to attention when I use that tone, but not my mate.

She fights with renewed fervor. At the rate she's going, she's going to hurt herself before she tires herself out, so I do the only thing I can think of to calm her.

I tilt her head to the side and bite her neck, gently but firmly.

It works. She gasps and goes completely still in my arms, surrendering to my dominance.

A surge of victory swells in my chest. Her submission, no matter how begrudgingly given, is oh so sweet, and I can't help the growl that rumbles up out of my chest, nor can I resist the urge to kiss and suck on the column of her throat.

She whimpers when I lave my tongue over her sensitive flesh. I feel the tremble go through her when I suck on it, urging all the blood to the surface so I can leave my mark on her.

I survey my handiwork with satisfaction when I'm done. Now when any male looks at her, he'll see that she belongs to me. My cock is still hard. The beast inside me is still raging at me to claim her fully, but this will placate him for the time being until I can make Mya mine fully.

Her face is flushed, and her eyes are still wild. She's already plotting a way to escape, and while part of me aches at the thought of my mate wanting to escape me so badly, another part of me is amused and even pleased. My mate is no pushover. She's a fighter.

Still, I don't need her fighting me right now. Not until I get her safely back to my compound where I can keep her contained.

I had anticipated the possibility of a fiery mate and came prepared.

"I'm sorry about this, little hellcat," I apologize to her before I press the needle into her neck too quickly for her to protest.

Her mouth drops open, and her eyes flare with betrayal before they flutter closed, and she slumps in my arms.

I catch her against my chest and lift her in my arms, brushing her silky curls back from her face as I cradle her against me.

She feels so right, so perfect in my arms. A rush of protectiveness courses through me.

"Don't worry, my love," I murmur down to her even though she can't hear me. "You're going to be the most treasured mate in the universe."

Mya

I wake up slowly, blinking several times as my eyes adjust to the brightness of the sunlight shining in through the window—a window that's not mine.

Suddenly, Raoul's golden eyes are peering into mine, and I sit up in a panic, my heart hammering against my rib cage, as everything comes crashing back to me.

"Whoa, be careful, little hellcat." Raoul reaches out a hand to steady me as the room spins.

"You drugged me," I hiss at him.

He hands me a bottle of water and instructs me, "Drink."

I take it and begrudgingly do as he says. It's only because my throat is parched and I'm insanely thirsty. If not for that, I'd have tossed the bottle back in his handsome face.

A shifter. Raoul is a freaking shifter, though what type I don't yet know.

I've heard about shifters, though I've never met one before—at least not that I knew of. They're animals—literally. Insanely strong and powerful and worse than a serial killer because at least with a serial killer, you're only dealing with a human. You have a tiny chance of escape. With a shifter, you have no chance of getting away. They're natural-born hunters. I remember the look of hunger in Raoul's eyes as he gazed down at me from his massive height. Predators.

"So what are you?" I ask him frankly.

Raoul just blinks at me, his golden eyes unwavering.

"You're a shifter," I prompt him. "What kind?"

When he doesn't immediately answer me, I add acidly. "Don't you think I have the right to know what type of animal the man who's captured me might suddenly morph into?"

He frowns at my tone, but he stands from where he's perched on the side of the bed, his muscles rippling and cording as he straightens to his full height. The man is insanely attractive. It's not fair.

He smirks at me as if he can read the direction of my thoughts, and I flush angrily, glaring at him.

"Why don't I just show you?" he proposes.

Before I can utter a word, he suddenly morphs before my very eyes. It happens so quickly I can hardly register it before an enormous tiger is standing on all fours before me.

And oh my god, he's beautiful.

I can see the sandy blonde color of his hair in his fur. It fades into a creamy white. His black stripes are bold and proud. My eyes trail down to his enormous paws as he pads across the room over to me.

His head is huge, and I feel a moment of surre-ality. I'm in a room with a tiger. A freaking tiger!

When he's standing by the bed, he's at eye level with me, and I instantly recognize his golden eyes are those of Raoul, the man.

I expel the breath I didn't realize I was holding, and against my better judgement, I reach out a hand to touch his fur. I don't plan it. It's like my hand moves of its own volition without permission from my brain. I'm helpless to stop it.

Raoul's eyes flicker closed when I touch him. His fur is soft underneath my fingertips, and I lightly stroke his head like I would a big cat.

I jump when a rumble sounds from his throat. Holy shit, he's purring!

I snatch my hand back and swallow. Raoul's eyes snap open, pinning me in his predatory gaze, and then he morphs back into his human state in the blink of an eye so that I'm staring at eye level with his very large, very aroused male body part. I can see the huge bulge of it in his slacks.

My face flames, and I avert my gaze. God, did me stroking his head like that turn him on that much?

"I've never let anyone pet me like that," his deep voice rumbles.

I look up at him. He doesn't look angry, though. His eyes are soft as he gazes down at me.

"Why did you let me?" I ask, though I suspect I already know what he's going to say.

He drops on his haunches before me, and I can still see a bit of the tiger in him as he runs his thumb along my bottom lip, his touching sending tingles shooting throughout my entire body.

"Because you're my mate, and there's not much I would deny you."

My throat goes dry as I stare at him. "How about giving me my freedom, then?" I challenge him.

His lips press into a thin line. He doesn't dignify that with a response. Instead, he straightens to his full height, and I think I see a flash of hurt in his eyes before he turns his back on me.

"I have some business to attend to. Rest, and I'll be back with food for you shortly," he orders me before he exits the room.

Of course, I hop out of bed as soon as the door clicks shut, and of course, the fucker is locked. I expected no less.

That still doesn't stop the disappointment from crashing through me.

I'm effectively trapped by a tiger, and while he might say I'm his mate, we all know cats are notorious for playing with their food before they eat it.

And I have no intention of being his little mouse.

I'm pacing by the window, contemplating potential escape routes when the door opens again. I've already checked the window and not only is it shut fast, but I would surely fall to my death if I could get it open and jump out of it anyway. Either that or break an arm or leg.

I spin toward the door, my tongue ready to lash out at my captor, but the words die in my throat when I see a woman walking in with a tray in her hands. When Raoul said he would bring me food, I assumed he meant *he* would do it.

Still, seeing as how this is the first other person I've seen since he took me captive, excitement creeps over me. Plus, there's the encouraging fact that she's a woman.

I naturally appeal to her, hoping that she will sympathize with my plight. Women's solidarity and all that, you know.

"Oh, thank God!" I rush over to her as she lays the tray on a little table in the corner of the opulent space. "I'm here against my will. Raoul kidnapped me. Can you help me?"

The woman casts me a cool glance. Her eyes are a startling shade of green, and her hair is long and blonde. She's tall and gorgeous.

Instead of any ounce of empathy in her eyes,

her lip turns up into a sneer as she addresses me harshly, "Ungrateful little brat. You are not worthy of our king."

"King?" I blink and take a step back.

She drags her eyes up and down on my body with derision, and it's clear I'm found wanting. I bristle under her assessing gaze.

"It's a pity you're the one king Raoul is convinced is his mate." She draws herself to her full height, throwing her shoulders back and tilting her head up proudly. "What does a mere human know about our ways? He needs a strong tigress to help him lead."

Comprehension dawns on me as I realized this woman is a tiger shifter, and she undoubtedly wants to be Raoul's queen. I feel a stab of something that I don't even want to identify, but I shake it off because all I want is my freedom. *I* certainly don't want Raoul.

I let out a sarcastic laugh. "Well, then by all means, take him." I splay my hands at her. "I don't want to rule your pack. Let me go and you can have him."

Her eyes turn livid with rage as she hisses at me, "My point exactly! Tigers do not travel in packs. You are not worthy of our streak!"

I nod. "I agree with you, and newsflash. I don't want to be here either, lady. So why don't you just help me break out of here, and then you can live happily ever after and rule your little pack—" At her growl, I correct myself, "—streak, whatever you want to call it."

She rolls her eyes at me like I'm being a petulant child. "That is not how this works, you silly child. It doesn't matter if I remove you or not. Raoul has recognized you as his mate, and he will not easily let you go. What's done is done, so you might as well get used to it. I certainly will not risk my life for you."

I clench my teeth as I glare back at her and try again. "Please, if he takes me as his mate, it will be without my consent."

She just glares at me coldly.

"That is essentially rape," I hiss at her.

She shrugs at me nonchalantly, as if it couldn't concern her at all. So much for women's solidarity.

"Is there anything else you require?" she asks me in a dry, bored tone, making it clear she'd rather eat nails than be in this room with me.

"No," I hiss at her, still seething over the fact that this woman is not going to try to help me. *Of course, she's not really a woman*, I remind myself.

She's a shifter. One of *them*. Nothing more than a beast.

She saunters through the door, closing it behind her and locking me back inside.

I stomp over to the food and pick up the plate. I consider tossing it against the wall. No doubt the smash of the plate shattering would make me feel better, but I pause with the plate halfway raised, reconsidering. If I want to have any hope of getting out of here alive, I'll need to keep my strength up. Refusing to eat is only punishing me—not Raoul. It's obvious I won't beat any of his streak with physical strength, so I'll have to outsmart them if I want to escape out of here.

I settle down at the table and barely taste the food as I shovel it into my mouth, still deep in thought.

I have to find a way out of this mess. I just have to.

FOUR

Mya

Raoul slams the door behind him. When he finally comes storming back through it at the end of the day, it's evening. It's not completely dark out yet. The sky is dusky, signaling the going down of the sun. I've been staring out the window most of the day, deep in thought and watching the sun's transition through the so I can somewhat tell the time since there's no clock in this room.

Raoul prowls over to me in that predatory way of his, his gaze pinned intently on me. "Do not attempt to solicit members of my staff to help you escape again." His voice is a low growl, a warning, and I tilt my chin up and stare back at him defiantly.

Did he really expect me to just take this lying down and to not attempt escape? If he did, he's a fool. I don't say that though, figuring it's best not to bait the tiger too much at this point. "Let me go and we won't have that problem," I counter back to him.

He tenses up, and I can't help adding, "I will never submit to this."

A roar finally tears up from his throat, and he pounces on me, pulling me up from the chair I'm sitting in and slamming my back against the wall. He towers over me, his golden eyes blazing down at me as he presses himself against me. I can feel the hardness of his chest, stomach, and arms—and I most especially feel that bulging part of him pressing insistently against me as well.

Although it makes my heart hammer against my ribs like a bird trying to beat free of its cage, I force myself to hold his gaze defiantly. He brushes his fingertips over the mark he left on my neck. Yeah, I saw the hickey right off when I went into the bathroom. He made sure to put it near the front of my neck where I can't cover it unless I keep my hair hanging in front of my shoulders all the time, which drives me crazy, and I'm sure that was the entire purpose of it—to make sure the mark is clearly visible at all times.

His eyes flare with heat as he stares at the mark. He brings his mouth close to my ear as he whispers, "You will submit to me, Mya."

"Never," I spit back.

His eyes flare with challenge. "Oh, yeah?"

Before I can even process his intention, he smashes his lips down onto mine. I gasp at the suddenness of his lips pressing against mine, and he takes advantage of my surprise, thrusting his tongue past my parted lips.

He kisses me voraciously, hungrily, like he's a man dying of thirst and I'm the holy water he needs for life. His arms band around my back, and I'm completely engulfed in him. His scent washes over me. It's something clean and fresh and woodsy and masculine.

I melt against him against my will, and his arms tighten around me. My mind is screaming at me to fight back, but my body has other ideas. It's relaxing into his hold, and he groans as he thrusts himself against me, humping me through our clothing.

"Fuck, hellcat," he groans out. "Let me have you, Mya, my sweet mate," he whispers against my ear before he sucks on my neck, no doubt trying to leave more marks on me. My mind screams at me to resist this assault on senses simply because he's my kidnapper, but my body has other ideas. I feel a pulsing take root deep inside my core. I whimper at the sensation, and Raoul's lips latch back onto mine again, kissing me even more fiercely than before. He's kissing me so deeply that it's pushing all rational thought out of my head. I can't think. All I can do is feel the assault of his tongue tangoing with mine.

"Submit to me," he growls into my mouth. My body is screaming at me to say yes, but my mind is stubborn. "No," I breathe.

A frustrated growl tears up from his throat, and he humps me harder, positioning himself so his hard length is stroking directly between my thighs. He's dragging it over this spot that causes tingles to radiate throughout my entire body. My toes curl, and I feel myself arching up into him, wanting more of that delicious sensation. He gives it to me too, dragging his length up and down me over and over again.

I mewl with pleasure. I feel this pressure

building inside me, and I can't help it. I begin humping back against him.

"Motherfuck," he growls out as we continue to ride each other through our clothing. I cry out when he slams himself against me and grinds his hips one last time. That dam of pressure gives way in a torrent of pleasure so intense I grasp at him to keep myself from falling down as my knees turn to jelly and sparks fly behind my vision.

I cry out a high-pitched sound I never knew I was capable of making as muscles I didn't even know existed convulsed around air. Pleasure courses through my limbs, making them lifeless and heavy.

Raoul clutches me against his chest. "Yes, that's a good little kitten. Look at you fall apart so beautifully for me." He rains praises down on me before he finally groans deeply and reaches down between us, freeing his throbbing length from his pants. It springs up into his waiting hand, and my eyes widen as I look down at him. I barely get a glimpse of the head that's red and swollen and angry-looking before his hand is moving up and down so quickly it's a blur.

He tilts my chin up, forcing me to meet his eyes as he stares down at me intently, his gaze roving over my face until his breath stutters and he grunts. With a roar, he pulls my shirt up and liquid warmth begins to spurt onto my skin. He's marking me with his cum, and while that should repulse me, I feel another throb in between my legs. His swollen appendage is huge. He looks just as big *there* as he is everywhere else, and I'm so tiny. He looks like he would split me into if he tried to stick it inside me, and that shouldn't make me throb even more, but it does.

There's obviously something wrong with me.

We're both panting, and when our eyes meet again, there's something feral and possessive in his gaze. It causes my breath to hitch. I don't know what to say, so I remain silent and swallow hard.

Raoul leans down and presses a tender kiss against the top of my forehead, and for some reason, that innocent gesture has tears springing to my eyes. I look down, trying to hide my emotion from him, but he tilts my chin up, forcing me to meet his probing gaze. One of the tears escapes and flows down my cheek. His gaze softens as he wipes it gently away with his thumb. The look in his eyes is so tender that I feel more tears rushing to my eyes.

"Kitten," he calls me softly, and then I lose the

battle, and the tears begin cascading down my face.

He grabs the back of my head and pulls me to his chest as I break down into sobs. I go willingly, burying my face in his chest as his arms band around me. He strokes his hands over my hair and my back soothingly before he picks me up and cradles me against his big chest.

He carries me over to the bed and sits down against the headboard with me still cradled in his lap. He rocks me like a baby as he continues to stroke me and shower me with tender praises and sweet promises, things no one has ever said to me before. "Such a sweet little kitten. My perfect little mate. It's okay. You'll see. Everything is going to be okay from now on. I'm going to take care of you."

Strangely enough, Raoul's words calm me as I allow them to wash over me. My sobs eventually subside, but I continue to lie in his steady hold, tired and confused and emotionally spent, until I eventually drift off to sleep.

Raoul

· · ·

She's perfect, and my loins burn with even more fire for her after seeing how beautifully she fell apart in my arms. I want to feel her shattering on me like that with my cock deep inside her.

Seeing my fierce little hellcat reduced to a purring kitten fills me with a sense of satisfaction like none other, and the emotion that poured out of her afterward only endeared her to me further and made me that much more protective and possessive of her. I want to shelter her from everything.

It's hard for me to pry myself away from her, but I eventually do. The duties of my kingdom call. Still, she's there in my mind in everything I do now. I'm impatiently awaiting the end of my duties so I can return to her.

When I finally do return to her, eager to see her beautiful face once more, she's guarded and pensive.

"Hello, kitten," I greet her warmly.

Her eyes trail over me warily. She doesn't speak. She just watches me apprehensively. She's no doubt confused and beating herself up over her reaction to me.

That's why, even though everything within me is screaming at me to push for more, I don't. I simply crawl into bed with her, pull her to my chest, wrap my arms and legs around her, and hold her close.

At first, she stiffens in my hold when she feels my hardness pressing up against her ass. I fight back a groan as she tries to wiggle away. I tighten my arms around her, holding her still before her, the friction of her ass sliding up and down my cock has me creaming in my boxers.

"Sleep," I whisper in her ear before I toy with a couple of the tendrils framing her neck. I feel the tremble go through her, and smile. She feels our connection too, try as she might to deny it.

When she realizes I'm not going to push for more tonight, she finally relaxes. I feel a sting of disappointment, but I fight it down. Holding her like this is enough for now. I can be content with just feeling her in my arms and knowing she's here.

For now.

Mya

For all Raoul's intensity that first day, he toned it down a notch for the rest of the week after he humped against me like a wild beast and forced an orgasm out of me, bringing me to the brink of total meltdown.

Although he backed off his, his blazing eyes are no less intense, but he leaves me every day to go do whatever it is tiger kings do, and when he returns home every night, he speaks a few cordial words to me before climbing into the bed and gathering me to his chest. He bands those arms and legs around me, effectively caging me in. I'd be lying if I said that his big body behind mine hasn't become comforting. I think I'm getting the best night's sleep I've ever had.

I should be worried about my rent, my job, and everything that I have waiting for me in my life back home, but I'm not. Keeping my wits about me in this strange place keeps me preoccupied.

It's strangely freeing to not have to worry about my bills and all of that.

Instead, I worry about when Raoul is going to make a move on me again and make my body betray me. He hasn't done more than hold me and kiss my forehead or the side of my neck since that first day, and I'm a confusing mix of relieved and disappointed at that.

I've given up on the thought of escape for now because I'm always locked in here. While Raoul's gone, the only person who ever comes in here other than him is Liza, the snarky tigress who obviously loathes me, there's no help there.

Now, I'm just biding my time. When I'm in this room alone all day, I read some of the books that Raoul has on a little shelf in the corner of the room. There's no TV or modern technology, no way for me to make contact with the outside world.

If I'm being totally honest, I don't have anyone to contact anyway other than the police maybe, but how much help would they really be? Our human police force is notorious for backing down when it comes to enforcing anything with shifters. They don't want to get involved with them because they know the shifters are way stronger than them and that it's a pointless fight. I certainly don't think they would stick their necks out on the line for insignificant little old me.

Besides, oddly enough, I'm falling into a kind of routine. Raoul gets up and leaves, and I take my time soaking in his luxurious bath, pampering my skin more than I ever have in my entire life. I brush my curls until they shine. There's a whole closet full of clothing stocked for me. It still trips me out when I walk into his huge walk-in closet and see a whole side of it dedicated to me. It's obvious Raoul really thinks I'm his mate. If I didn't already know how serious he was about that claim, then seeing the mountains of clothes he had brought in and packed into the closet next to his is more than enough proof Raoul doesn't intend on ever letting me go.

That doesn't feel me with quite as much panic as it used to, and I'm seriously thinking that when I do get out of here, I'm going to need lots and lots of psychological therapy. I definitely need to have my brain checked to make sure that I'm normal because something's not right. I should be panicking more than I am right now. In fact, I'm actually becoming comfortable in his opulent space—and maybe that's all it is. As a girl who grew up with hardly anything, maybe it's just the comfort of his luxury suite that's charming me into complacency. And maybe that was his plan all along—to charm his victims into complacency with all of these creature comforts, and then he'll make his move.

My heart hammers wildly in my chest when I remember the way he snarled as he shot his seed all over my stomach, and I can't help imagining how it would feel to feel that hot liquid spurting up inside me.

My cheeks flame as I think about it, and I feel a throbbing between my legs. I clench my legs together, trying to ease the ache, but it doesn't help. I bite my lip and consider. I've never been one of those girls who could make herself come. Sure, I've tried to touch myself before, but I never could reach that pinnacle, but now I know what it feels like. Now I know what to look for after what Raoul did to me, so maybe I can achieve it on my own?

I slip my hand up under the little sundress I'm wearing. Raoul seems to prefer his mate to wear dresses because that's practically all he stocked the closet with. I don't know if it's because he just likes the way I look in dresses or if it's because he theoretically wants to have easy access to me in case he does decide to make good on his threat and make me his mate in *every* way.

Regardless of the reason, I have to admit that I like the way the material feels flowing down over my skin. I slip my hand into the band of my panties. My face flushes again as I think of how even my undergarments are now provided by Raoul. I wonder if he picked them out himself. The lacy options make me think either he did choose them himself or he instructed someone what he wanted bought.

My tiger seems to prefer his women in lace undergarments and pretty little dresses.

I still when I realized I just thought of Raoul as *my* tiger. I scowl, but it doesn't stop the insistent throbbing between my legs, so with a frustrated groan, I continue to slip my fingers in between my legs until I find that little bundle of nerves that sends tingles shooting throughout my entire frame when I press on it.

I can't hold in the little moan that escapes me as I begin to rub it in circles, imagining that it's Raoul's hard length pressing against me, humping against me. I recall the way his body felt that day, and I remember his feral grunts and groans, his intoxicating smell.

My breathing becomes shallower as I rub harder and faster. I feel that pressure within me building, and just as I feel like I'm on the precipice of coming, I whisper his name, "Raoul."

Suddenly, my hand is yanked from between my legs, and both of my hands are pinned above my head. My wrists are banded between two big paws. My eyes fly open, and my flush only deepens when I see Raoul's golden eyes blazing down into me. His chest is heaving up and down as he growls at me, "Do you know what it does to me to walk in here and see you touching your pretty little pussy while moaning out my name?"

I don't have a chance to answer before he smashes his lips down onto mine. Oh god, I must have been so deep into what I was doing that I didn't hear him come in. but my flush of mortification quickly fades into nothingness whenever his lips claim mine so ferociously. He kisses me so fiercely that my brain short circuits and I forget to feel embarrassment or anything. I can't think at all. All I can do is gyrate my hips against his as he humps me. I whimper. I *need* to come.

Raoul finally pulls his lips back from mine. When they're just a hair's breadth from mine, he whispers, "Your pleasure is mine. If you need to come, you tell *me* and *I* will do it."

Something about the way he says that so adamantly, like he's berating me for seeking my own pleasure, causes fire to lick throughout my veins.

"Does my little kitten need to come?" Raoul purrs down at me knowingly.

I'm beyond the point of shyness or coyness. I hear myself shamelessly tell him, "Yes."

He stops pumping me and starts moving off of me. I let out a whimper of protest, my eyes flying open.

"Relax, Mya. I'm going to give you what you need," he assures me. He strokes a hand over my stomach as he crawls in between my legs.

My brow is furrowed when he settles in

between my thighs and pulls my panties to the side. He looks up at me wickedly before he kisses me down *there*. It's an open-mouth kiss, and the feeling of his tongue sliding over my sensitive flesh has me arching up into him and fisting his hair.

I can't believe he's doing this, but I'm powerless to stop him. He holds me still with his hands on either side of my hips as he feasts on me. He brings me closer and closer to the edge before backing off and then building it all back up over again. I'm writhing and panting and begging and sobbing, "Please, Raoul, please."

"Who do you belong to?" Raoul prompts me.

I don't answer. I just whine and toss my head on the pillow.

He stops licking me altogether and crawls up until his face is mere inches from mine. I look up into his eyes wildly. My juices are glittering on his mouth and chin. "Who's mate are you?" His eyes are a golden fire, and I'm burning in them.

I bite my lip and look down, not wanting to admit it, but desperate for the pleasure that only he can give me. He grabs my chin and holds my eyes captive. His golden orbs blaze into me knowingly. "Say it, Mya," he orders, looking every inch one-hundred percent alpha male, and I can't deny it any longer.

"Yours!" I scream. "I'm yours!" The words come tumbling out of me in a rush as tears spring to my eyes. Damn it. How does Raoul always make me *feel* so much?

"That's a good kitten," he praises me before he goes back between my legs. He has my body detonating with one perfectly placed lick. I scream as white-hot pleasure pulses throughout my entire body. It's more intense than the first orgasm he gave me. It's so intense I can't breathe as I skyrocket onto another planet.

When I come back down to earth, he has gathered me in his arms. He's stroking my hair and raining praises down upon me. I feel weak, like I just ran a 5K marathon.

I ignore the part of my brain that's telling me I shouldn't cuddle into my captor like this. Instead, I curl myself around him and settle my head on his chest. I close my eyes and savor the feeling of his big arms around me as I fall asleep.

SIX

Raoul

Mya is mine. She admitted it last night, and there's no way I'm going to allow her to take it back. My cock hardens, demanding that I claim her here and now, but I straighten my collar instead, my eyes flicking in the mirror to take in Mya as she slips on a floor-length, sky-blue dress. The satin ripples over her gentle curves, and the low back dips down almost to the top of her ass. It's clear she's not wearing a bra underneath it with her entire back exposed like that, and I growl as I walk over to her and unpin her hair.

"Hey!" she protests as the curls go tumbling down her back in a shimmer of golden red. "I spent a long time on perfecting that updo!"

"I like it better like this," I tell her. I catch her eyes in the mirror. She flushes when I level my heated gaze on her. I truly do prefer her hair down and wild about her shoulders like this. It doesn't hurt that it covers some of her delectable skin from prying male eyes. Of course, no one in my streak would dare to look at my mate the wrong way, but I'm not taking any chances. No need to tempt them.

While still holding her eyes, I pull her hair back over her shoulder and lean down to press a kiss against the nape of her neck. I feel her tremble in my arms. She bites her lip as she leans back against me. I wrap an arm around her waist and pull her back flush to my chest, pressing my erection into her sweet ass so she can feel exactly what she does to me.

She hangs onto my arm that's banded around her waist as I suck on the side of her neck, needing to visibly mark her since I can't sheathe myself inside her and claim her right now.

She doesn't understand the significance of tonight's event. I merely told her we were having an event and that I wanted her to accompany me as my date. She doesn't know that the event in question is to celebrate *her*.

My mate. My queen.

It's no matter. She'll find out soon enough, and hopefully she doesn't make a scene.

My lips quirk up at the corners as I pull back from her and survey my handiwork. On second thought, maybe I *want* her to make a scene. It would be good for the streak to see what a fierce little hellcat my mate can be, and the thought of her eyes flashing angrily makes my cock stiffen even more.

I pull back from her with a groan and adjust myself. They'll be time enough for that later because whether Mya realizes it or not, by admitting she's my mate, she's turned me into a ticking time bomb.

I will be claiming what's rightfully mine tonight.

"You look beautiful, kitten."

She flushes under my praise, and I smile. She will submit to me willingly tonight. Her body can't deny this pull between us even if her head wants to.

Mya is mine. Plain and simple.

At least a hundred pairs of eyes are on us as we descend the long, spiral staircase. The feeling of Mya's naked skin underneath my hand splayed across her back is warm and comforting. My chest puffs with pride at presenting my mate to my streak.

I look down at her lovingly. My beautiful little mate. She walks gracefully, floating down the staircase with her head held high, even if she does seem a bit shy with so many eyes on her.

She looks innocent and charming, but I know the fire that lays underneath the surface. She'll make a fine queen, and I'll be there to train her every step of the way.

Mya does well with the introductions. Though her eyes flash to me the first time I introduce her as my mate, she doesn't make a sound of protest. I pull her closer against my side and tighten my hold on her waist as she smiles at all the males who come up to greet her.

I'm insanely jealous, but I can't help it. I don't like seeing her smiling at other men like this, but I know she's just being polite. However, when my brother takes her hand and kisses the back of it, I can't stop the growl that tears up out of my throat.

His humorous grin as he glances at me lets me know he did it just to goad. The insufferable prick. "That is the first and last time your lips ever touch any part of my mate," I warn him.

He holds his hands up as he takes a step back. "Of course, your Grace." He winks at Mya, and she giggles.

I frown down at her, and she raises an eyebrow at me. "Do you have to be such a Neanderthal?"

I lean down so I can speak directly into her ear where no one else can hear, "You'd do well to try not to make me jealous, kitten."

She gapes up at me and sputters defensively, "I haven't done anything!"

"You in that dress, looking pretty enough to eat and smiling at all my men is more than enough to make me want to claim you right here and now in front of all of them just so they know exactly who you belong to," I warn her.

I'm pleased to see that her cheeks are flushed prettily when I pull back from her, and her breathing is uneven.

"You're insufferable," she breathes under her breath.

"And you are *mine*." I press her closer to my side.

The time has come for me to make my announcement. I pull Mya to the stage with me.

"What are you doing?" she hisses at me, but I ignore her. There's no way I'm giving her a heads-up or a way out of this now. Better to just spring it on her in front of everyone. She already knows the truth anyway.

"Smile," I order her before I pull her onto the stage steps.

She looks like she'd rather claw my eyes out, and that makes my cock harden, but she pastes a pretty smile on her face instead, no doubt only because there are so many eyes on us up here.

"Ladies and gentleman," I begin, and a hush falls over the streak. "It is with great pleasure that I officially present to you my mate and your new queen, Mya."

Mya's face turns red, and I feel her gaze boring a hole into the side of my head. Just as the crowd erupts into cheers, a roaring voice booms out, "Over my dead body!"

I frown, wondering who would have the audacity to challenge me. My eyes skate over the crowd until I find the source of the voice standing tall and proud in the back of the room.

A growl begins low in the back of my throat as we lock eyes and he strides purposefully toward the stage.

I push Mya protectively behind me, guarding her with my body as the lion king makes his way to the stage with murder in his eyes.

What the fuck is he doing here?

"Get your filthy paws off my daughter!" he roars as he leaps onto the stage.

"I don't know what you're playing at, lion king, but—"

"Daughter?" Mya's confused voice cuts into the conversation. I growl as I feel her step out from behind me.

Lionel's eyes dart to her and soften as they take her in. "That's right, child. You're my daughter."

Mya shakes her head as she adamantly voices, "No, you're mistaken. I never knew my father, and my mother died years ago, and I'm just a human."

Lionel sighs heavily before he confesses. "Your mother and I were in love, but my pack would never accept her. I didn't know she was pregnant. She ran away from me. I didn't find out about you until years later, and by then, I didn't want to upend your whole life, especially if I knew my pack would never accept you if you couldn't shift."

He looks at her with new hope in his eyes. "You haven't shifted into your lioness form yet, have you?"

Mya stares at him as she shakes her head numbly. "No, I told you. I'm just a human. This isn't true. This can't be true. My mother never spoke about my father. He was off-limits."

"Why do you think that is, child?" Lionel asks her gently.

Mya's eyes rove over him again, and my own eyes flicker back and forth between the pair, noting the resemblances I wish weren't there. She's got the man's stubborn chin, the same shape to her eyes, though hers are blue whereas his are a deep brown. I take in her fiery red curls that wave down around her in a glorious mane. She looks exactly like a fierce little lioness. I don't know how I didn't see it before.

The truth hits me square in the chest. Mya is the daughter of my sworn enemy. A lioness, though she's never shifted, so she must have more human blood in her than lion.

I wait for the crushing sensation of knowing

she's my enemy's blood to overtake me, but it doesn't happen. I blink as I realize this changes nothing.

Mya is still *mine*. My mate. My queen. My everything. And I'll be damned if I let this pretentious ass take her away from me.

Mya doesn't say anything. She's still staring at Lionel uncertainly, but he steps toward her and holds out a hand. "Come now, daughter. Let me take you home where you belong, what I should have done all those years ago, whether you could shift or not."

I growl menacingly as I step back in front of Mya protectively, positioning myself between her and her father.

Lionel's eyes light with fire, and a growl rumbles up out of his throat as well. I don't give a fuck. "You're not taking her anywhere. Mya is my mate."

Lionel's eyes go wild at the word "mate," and then he's launching himself at me with a roar, his body shifting midair.

I immediately shift as well and jump forward to meet him.

We're snarling and roaring and growling and tearing at each other with our paws. I howl as he lands a scratch on my shoulder, but I get it right across the face, causing him to screech and stumble back. He shakes his head before tearing into me again.

I can feel the pulsing energy from my streak. They want to jump in and intervene, but I mentally tell them no, that this fight is mine. There is no honor in an entire streak ganging up on one lion. No, I will fight Lionel into submission on my own and prove myself worthy of his daughter.

Mya screams. Her sound of distress distracts me and sends fear racing through me. I instinctively glance over at her to make sure she's okay, and that's when I feel it. Lionel tackles me to the ground and holds my neck down. He'll be going in for the kill any minute now, and all I can think about is what's going to happen to Mya without me there to protect her.

"No!" I hear Mya scream, and then suddenly another furry body crashes into us, knocking Lionel off me.

I hear a collective gasp go up from the crowd, and when I look up to see what happened, my breath catches in my throat.

The most beautiful tigress I've ever seen positions herself between Lionel and me. Her fur is a beautiful white striped with black, but her mane is a glorious red. I suppose "tigress" might not be the right term for her. She's a beautiful mix between a tiger and a lion. A liger.

She's standing with her back to me, snarling at Lionel. She's *protecting* me, and my heart swells as I jump to my feet and stand next to her, positioning myself slightly in front of her, protecting her back.

I see the shock in Lionel's eyes as she stares at Mya. I look at her too, seeing that it's indeed her beautiful blue eyes staring stubbornly at her father as she stands between him and me, siding with *me*, choosing *me*.

Knowing that my mate is willing to risk her own life for me is doing funny things to me. I'm horny as hell, and it takes everything in me not to mount her here and now in front of everyone.

The three of us continue to stare one another down until Lionel finally shifts back to his human form in resignation. Only when he does do Mya and I do likewise.

Mya has a shocked look on her face as she holds her hands up and looks at them with a furrow in her brow.

"I take it that's the first time you've ever shifted, kitten?" I ask her gently.

She looks up at me dazedly and nods.

I pull her close to me and kiss her forehead tenderly. "It took thinking your mate was in danger to pull it out of you."

She opens up her mouth as if to argue, but then she closes it and buries her head in my chest. I wrap my arms around her possessively, aware that the entire streak is still watching this entire exchange with bated breath—as is her father.

"Well, I...I never—" Lionel sputters.

I interrupt him with, "As you can clearly see, Mya is my one true mate." I cast eyes out over my streak as well, speaking to them just as much as I am to her father. I heard the murmurings among my streak that Mya wouldn't be fit to rule them since she was merely human. Well, now they see that's she's a shifter too. They also see the lengths she'll go to in order to protect one of her own.

I see several of my men nod, and many of the females are holding their hands over their mouths with tears glistening in their eyes. Mya's selfless actions have earned their respect, and pride for my mate wells up within me. "If you'll excuse us, though, the events of tonight have taxed her, so I'm going to see her to bed."

I bend and lift Mya into my arms, cradling her against my chest. She keeps her head buried against me. Whether she's seeking comfort from me or just hiding her face out of embarrassment, I don't know, but I revel in the feeling of her burrowed into me.

My subjects bow their heads to me as I pass by. I turn back when I reach the doors and tell Lionel. "I expect to see you here in the morning. We have much to discuss."

The lion king merely nods his head in deference, looking shocked and defeated.

I don't worry about all of that now. I'll deal with him tomorrow. Right now, claiming my mate is the only thing on my mind.

CHAPTER

SEVEN

Mya

I'm still reeling from everything that happened tonight when Raoul carries me over the threshold to his bedroom and kicks the door shut behind us.

I'm a shifter. A lioness. Or a tiger. Or a mixture of both. Hell, I don't know what I am.

But what's obvious is that everything Raoul has been telling me is true. There's no use fighting it now. I am indeed his mate. When I saw my father's jaws hovering over Raoul's neck, ready to strike, I didn't think. I just reacted, throwing myself between them in order to save Raoul.

I couldn't bear the thought of never seeing his golden eyes blazing down at me again, and in that moment, I didn't even stop to think about what that might mean.

But when Raoul sits me gently on the bed and squats down before me, tilting my chin up to force me to meet his gaze, I know that I'm going to have to think about it now.

"You know you are mine," his voice purrs as his eyes rove over my face adoringly.

The way he's looking at me, coupled with that slight purr in his voice, has me trembling.

"Raoul…" I begin, but he pulls my hands up to his lips and kisses them reverently.

"You put yourself in danger for me." His accusation comes out half wonder, half admonition.

I swallow before admitting, "I couldn't let him kill you."

Raoul's golden eyes stare into mine worshipfully before he kneels before me and lowers his head in a bow. "My queen."

My breath hitches at his show of submission. I already know that as the tiger king Raoul has never submitted to anyone, yet here he is on his knees, bowing to *me*.

Something inside me breaks. It's like all the ice

surrounding my heart thaws and melts away to be replaced by a burning heat. My entire body relaxes, and I lean into him. "Raoul," I say his name, my voice breaking at the end, and that's all it takes for my mate to rise and take me in his arms.

He crushes me to his chest and devours me. He kisses all over my face, my cheeks, my forehead, and my lips before he begins moving down by throat. He slides the straps of my dress off and takes my nipples in between his teeth, sending electric shocks shooting throughout my entire system. He kisses every inch of my skin he can find, coming up periodically to drink from my lips again.

"Fuck, Mya. My perfect mate. My queen. I adore you. I worship you," he whispers against my skin in between licks and sucks. He's sucking on me like he wants to leave hickeys all over my body, and at this point, I don't even care. I'll wear all his marks with pride.

"Raoul," I moan out. "Please, I need you." I tell him as I arch my hips up into him, rubbing myself against his swollen flesh through our clothing.

Raoul makes a strangled noise before he sits me up and yanks the dress over my head, flinging it to the floor. He does likewise with his own clothing until we're sitting before each other on the bed naked.

His eyes rake over my nakedness, and I fight the urge to cover myself with my arms. This is Raoul, my mate, and it's obvious from the way he's looking at me I have nothing to be insecure about.

"So beautiful," he murmurs before his lips descend on mine again. He continues to kiss me as he presses me back against the bed. He cages me in with his big arms on other side of me. He's leaning on his elbows as he settles his weight on me, and I feel that swollen part of him prodding against my opening.

"Fuck, kitten, feel how wet you are for me?" He closes his eyes and drags his length against me a couple of times, hitting my clit and sending pleasure rocketing through me.

I moan and lift my hips up to him in invitation, my entire body throbbing, wanting to be filled by him.

He growls when he sees my offering and sits back to position himself at my opening.

I close my eyes at the sting as he starts to press into me.

"Eyes on me, kitten," he growls. I open my eyes

obediently to find his blazing golden orbs trained intently on me as he continues to push into me. His jaw is tight, and sweat beads his brow. The muscles in his arms flex as he pushes into me inexorably slowly. I can tell it's costing him to hold back.

And suddenly, I don't want him to hold back. I need him to take me roughly.

"Take me," I urge him as I wrap my arms and legs around him, digging my heels into his ass to urge him forward.

The muscles of my pussy clench involuntarily around him, and he curses before he slams the rest of the way inside me.

I feel the barrier of my innocence give way as he shreds my virginity in two. "Raoul!" I scream his name, but he swallows my cry with a desperate kiss. His tongue twines with mine. He kisses me breathless as he begins to move inside me, slamming his huge girth and length in and out of me.

I feel that delicious pressure building, but it's building deeper than ever before. "You feel that?" Raoul pants against my neck as he fists my hair. "That's me mating you. You are mine now, Mya. Mine. Always and forever. With any luck, I'll breed you with the big load I've got brewing just for you, kitten."

His words shouldn't turn me on the way they do, but they do. My muscles clench around him involuntarily, and he moans gutturally.

"Yes, that's it, kitten. Keep milking me like that with those tight little muscles, and I'm going to give it all to you."

He continues to stroke inside me, harder and faster now. "Raoul!" I scream out his name as he hits this spot inside me that causes me to see stars.

"Yes! That's it, kitten! Give it to me!" He encourages me as he stabs that spot over and over again.

I cling to him as I shatter, my mouth opening in a silent scream as my entire body convulses. I may have died. I'm not sure. If it's possible to die from pleasure, then I'm definitely dead. I close my eyes as the white-hot heat rushes over me.

Raoul roars my name, and then I feel him pumping his release into me. His cock is pulsing inside me as he gathers me tight to his chest and buries his face in my hair, his entire body trembling with the force of his spasms.

I don't know how long we lay there clinging to each other, but when I become aware of my surroundings again, Raoul has arranged me so that I'm laying right on top of him. "There you are, kitten," he tells me as my eyes flutter open and focus on him.

"Hi," I tell him softly.

He grins that heart-stopping crooked smile of his. "Hey, hellcat."

I purse my lips as I prop my head on my head and gaze down at him. "Is it hellcat or kitten?"

His handsome face breaks out into a full smile as he chuckles. "Both, mate. It's both. My hellcat on the streets and my kitten in the sheets."

I lay my head back on his chest to hide my smile.

Yeah, I guess I can live with that.

"I love you, Mya, my queen," his deep voice rumbles right underneath my ear.

I tilt my head up to meet his eyes as I tell him what I know he longs to hear. "I love you too, Raoul, my king."

His golden eyes blaze with renewed heat as he kisses me again.

And I do. I love him. Raoul. My kidnapper. My mate. My tiger king.

EPILOGUE

Six Months Later

Raoul

My entire body responds as I hear my wife's laughter floating over to me. I glance over to her where she's sitting with a few of the other tigresses in our streak. After she fearlessly defended me in front of everyone, they accepted her as one of their own. Even Liza warmly greets her now with a hug and a kiss on her cheek, and it was my understanding that she and the alpha tigress got off on the wrong foot.

I turn my attention back to the tigers and lions at my table. I never thought I would see the day that our streak and their pack would be enjoying a meal together, but here we are. I can't exactly say the tigers and lions are still the best of friends, but our respective communities have formed a sort of alliance, and it's all because of Mya.

Despite the man's shortcomings, the lion king truly does seem to care about his daughter and wants to be a part of her life. He was so desperate to be in her life that he was willing to agree to practically any terms I laid for us.

And I have to respect that.

I glance over at Mya again, my eyes stroking over her gently swollen belly. I already know I'll feel just as protective of our little cub as I am Mya—especially if it's a girl.

Mya catches me looking at her and smiles at me saucily. She tosses her head, and her red curls go bouncing down her back. The little minx. She knows exactly what she's doing. She knows that mane of red hair drives me wild. I love nothing more than to sit her in my lap and have her ride me while I suck on her pretty little titties and watch that hair bounce all around her shoulders. It's wild and untamed, just like her.

My mate rarely wants a gentle fuck. Even though I call her "kitten," she's a fierce little hellcat in the bedroom, too. She likes it rough and dirty. Sometimes I'm afraid I'll hurt her with my aggression, but she always screams for me.

She casts another flirty glance my way, and I harden my jaw. That's not the only thing on me that's hard. The appendage between my legs is so swollen I literally ache with need.

I excuse myself from the table and head over to where the tigresses and lionesses are assembled. Liza elbows Mya in the ribs knowingly as I walk up behind them, and Mya looks up at me with feigned wide-eyed innocence, as if she doesn't know by now that this would be the reaction to her baiting me across the room.

"If you ladies will excuse us, I need a moment alone with my wife," I say as I pull Mya up from the table without waiting for an answer.

The women titter and giggle, no doubt already knowing what's in store for their queen as I drag her down the hallway. I can't even make it to our room. Instead, I find an abandoned alcove and thrust her up against the wall.

"Naughty little kitten," I breathe down at her as I yank down her dress and free those perfect little breasts. They're swollen beautifully in her pregnancy, and I can't get enough of them. I lean down and suck on one as she arches her back up to me.

"I don't know what you're talking about," she denies in a silky voice.

My fingers find their way under her dress. I push aside her panties and plunge two fingers inside her. She's soaking wet, so I slip in easily. "Motherfucker. Your sweet little kitty is weeping for me," I groan against her skin.

"Raoul," she moans, all pretenses gone. I know exactly how to make my mate detonate. All it takes is a few calculated swirls of my thumb across her clit, and she's soaking my hand with moisture as she bites down against my shoulder to keep from screaming out so the entire dining hall doesn't hear what we're doing.

I claim her lips in a searing kiss, marveling at the way she tastes just as sweet as she did the first time. "So damn perfect. Every damn time," I whisper against her lips in between kisses. My cock feels like it's about to burst through my zipper. With a groan, I reach down and release it with one hand as I lift Mya's ass with the other. She willingly wraps her arms and legs around me as I position myself at her entrance and then slide in in one clean thrust.

We moan in unison, and I don't even try to be gentle. I rear my hips back until I'm nearly all the way out before I slam up inside her again.

Mya curses, and that only makes my blood boil hotter. "Whose are you?" I demand.

"Yours," she answers me breathlessly.

It doesn't matter how many times I've had my mate, my claiming is just as possessive and obsessive as always. If I thought I was obsessed with her before, it's only magnified a hundredfold since I've had her. Every time I have her, it only makes me want more. It doesn't lessen the need at all. It just makes it that much more intense.

"Who's the only one that can make this little kitty purr like this?"

Mya doesn't answer me right away. She's got her head thrown back, her eyes closed to sensation. I take the opportunity to suck on the creamy column of her throat, leaving another mark since my previous one has faded.

I slow down my thrusts, and she lets out a whimper of protest. I tilt her chin to me and prompt her again, "Who?"

"You!" she half growls, half screams in a mixture of frustration and desire.

"Damn right," I tell her before I begin to pound up into her harder and faster, giving her what she needs. I want to feel her pussy fluttering all over me when I come inside her.

"Raoul!" she screams my name as she convulses around me.

My breath stutters as I unload myself deep inside her, groaning at the way my seed rips out of my balls and tears up my stalk. It's so intense I almost pass out as I stand there, my chest heaving as I fight for breath.

Mya's little chest is panting up and down too as she goes lax in my arms.

"How do you get better and better every time?" I ask her.

She grins up at me before she teases, "I'm just good like that."

I laugh and kiss her soundly, "Yes, you are," I agree. "You're perfect."

She smiles up at me, and her smile is so radiant it takes my breath away. She lights up my entire world. In Mya, I found more than my mate. I found my other half, my queen, my soulmate—and I'm never going to let her go. It's my mission to make her purr for the rest of our days. I might be the tiger king, but I bow to my fiery little queen.

Hey there, you gorgeous reading machine!

First of all, THANK YOU for spending your precious time with my characters and letting me take up space in your brain for a while. You could've been doing literally anything else—like scrolling social media or alphabetizing your spice rack—but instead, you chose this. And I love you for it.

Now, let me let you in on a little secret: I'm basically the romance writing equivalent of a shapeshifter. One author, multiple personalities. Here are the pen names I write under:

- Emma Bray — steamy contemporary romance that's all heart eyes and heat
- Kenzie Skye — spicy romantasy and paranormal goodness—magic, monsters, and all the feels

- DAHLIA — downright filthy, dirty, naughty erotic romance (It's okay if you like it. I won't tell. 🫢)
- E.B. Fox — dark, broody, edge-of-your-seat romance for when you want to walk on the wild side

Craving more? Head to www.spicy-romance.com and sign up for my newsletter. As a thank-you, you'll get a free book you can't find anywhere else. (Check out this preview to get a sample of it.)

And I promise, cross my heart and swear on my sexiest plot twist: I will NEVER spam you. Only juicy updates, exclusive goodies, and sneak peeks that'll leave you begging for more.

Stay spicy, stay amazing, and keep chasing those happily ever afters (or wickedly dark ones— no judgment).

Big hugs and even bigger love,

The romance writing shapeshifter

P.S. Did I mention you're awesome? Because you are. 🖤

P.S.S. Here are some super handy-dandy lists where you can find all of my books:

- books2read.com/rl/emmabray
- books2read.com/rl/kenzieskye
- books2read.com/rl/dahlia
- books2read.com/rl/ebfox

Keep reading for an excerpt from Stalked by the Vampire.

STALKED BY THE VAMPIRE

My nostrils flare, and my fangs press against my gums, threatening to descend.

I shake my head and try to clear the cloud of lustful hunger that's slowly curling its fingers around my mind like a slow fog creeping in.

It's obviously been too long since my last feeding.

A good feeding can last me for nearly a month, although to be in the best health, it's ideal if I feed every couple of weeks. I've had to refrain from my typical biweekly meal, though. I've been trying to make it as long as I can between feedings because too many suspicious deaths are turning up. Mortals become anxious when they see a pattern of deaths, all too eager to pronounce that they have a serial killer in their midst, and when they do that, the local police force will only amp up its vigilance, making it more difficult than ever to take a discreet kill.

And I'm nothing if not discreet. I always feed from the dregs of society, those that humans would be better off without.

It's not me or any of my subjects raising their suspicions. Other unnaturally violent deaths have been occurring throughout the city lately, and they all have the mark of others of my kind on them.

Until my men can find the rogues and get them all under control, we're all on a diet.

I clench my jaw tightly and try to focus.

I'm sure my eyes are morphing from their normal golden brown to a burnt copper color.

I inhale a deep breath, something my mortal self used to do when I needed to calm down.

You'd think after two centuries of being a vampire I'd know by now that same tactic doesn't work on my immortal self.

No, it only draws the scent of food even further into my nostrils and heightens my hunger.

I continue to fight the primal instinct to hunt, and just as I think I have it under control and feel my fangs retracting back up to where they belong, I get a whiff of something so sweet and flowery, it almost knocks me over with the potent surge of lust that roars through me.

My fangs fully descend, and my eyes glow red, sharpening my already heightened vision as all my senses home in on the source of the smell.

The scent is heady, a mixture of roses and lilies and lavender all rolled into one. It wraps around me like a boa constrictor, squeezing all self-control from me while intoxicating me all at once.

It smells *delicious*. It smells like *mine*.

Don't ask me why fucking flowers smell so mouth-watering to me as a vampire. I know it's odd. You'd think the scents that would tempt me the most would be ones that smelled like the savory human foods I used to love.

No, now I crave flowers.

The scent is getting closer now, so whomever it belongs to is walking this way.

My vision goes red as the scent assaults me so closely now. Without thought, I fling myself from the shadows and snatch the source of the sweet scent, dragging the body back into the darkened alley with me. I move with super-human speed, grabbing my prey so quickly it probably looks like someone has vanished into thin air.

I hear a tiny gasp and look down to see my capture is a woman. That sweet floral scent is overwhelming me now, and I'm dying for a taste.

Just as I begin to lower my head to drink from her sweet nectar, she turns her head up to look at me.

I'm almost physically knocked back by the most innocent-looking pair of blue eyes I've ever seen in my life. They're framed by thick lashes, and instead of screaming at the monster looming over her, ready to end her life, she's looking up at me curiously, her mouth open in a little "o."

She's a tiny thing. The top of her head barely reaches my chest. My eyes sweep over her, and my chest tightens.

She's fucking beautiful.

Her hair is a golden blond that rivals the glory of the morning sunshine. Her skin is smooth and flawless and pulsing with beautiful, vibrant life.

And her lips...they're a puffy pink. The sight of them parted ever so slightly sends a surge of desire rushing through me.

I become aware of how small she is in my hold. My entire hand almost spans the width of the small of her back. Her little chest is heaving up and down, drawing my eyes to the slight cleavage revealed by the top two buttons of her white blouse. My eyes trail down further to take in the black skirt she's wearing.

My mind instantly puts two and two together. She's a waitress from the fancy joint just a couple of blocks up. I've "eaten" there many a time. How have I never seen this beautiful little angel before?

And that's what she is. An angel sent down from heaven. I'm suddenly filled with shame and self-loathing. This woman is young. She barely looks legal. She's pure and beautiful and innocent, and who am I to taint her with my touch?

She doesn't deserve to be soiled by a monster like me, a devil too sinful even for the depths of hell.

With more self-control than I've ever exhibited, I pull back from her. Every muscle in my body is taut as I physically restrain myself from sinking both my fangs and my cock inside her.

I've never wanted anyone as much as I want this little mortal standing so fearlessly in front of me.

And it would be so easy to take her any way I want. But the thought of seeing that pure, vibrant life draining from her eyes makes me sick to my stomach. Like I'll have really and truly committed the worst sin.

It's ironic. I've killed thousands of people and never felt an ounce of remorse for it. I just saw it as doing what had to be done to sustain myself. Call it the food chain and survival of the fittest, if you will.

But somehow the thought of draining this precious girl of life makes me feel like I really would damn myself more than I already am.

"Who are you?" She speaks in a breathy whisper, and her voice is like the sweetest melody. It washes over me and pulls at something inside me that feels suspiciously like my heart, an organ I'd long since thought dead.

I don't answer her. Instead, I cup the side of her cheek, electricity shooting through me where my fingers make contact with her petal-soft skin.

My eyes capture hers, and I allow my power to wash over her.

Her eyelids flutter closed, and I'm already mourning the loss of the light those pretty blue eyes shined on me. I catch her to my chest as she slumps.

Unfortunately, I can't erase her memory of me,

but I can put her into a temporarily catatonic state.

I lift her into my arms effortlessly. I'm stronger than a mortal, but even without my unnatural strength, I can tell she weighs no more than a feather.

I can't resist stroking my hand over her cheek and testing the silky softness of that long blond hair that's falling over my arms.

A quick check of the identification she carries on her tells me where she lives. I summon my driver with a thought.

I look back down at her I.D. as I wait for my driver to show up.

Elena Martin. "Elena," I voice her name softly, tasting it on my tongue. My eyes rove over her face that's still just as beautiful in its peaceful slumber as it was when she was awake and staring up at me with wide eyes. The name suits her. *Elena.*

I finally hear James pull up. He knows better than to ask questions when I step out of the shadows with a woman's tiny frame cradled against my chest, so if he's curious about what I'm doing with her, he keeps his thoughts to himself.

I tell him the address and then raise the glass

separating him from us so I can stare down at her in privacy.

Her sweet scent is still surrounding me, and while it's no less difficult to keep myself from tasting her, I find the need to protect her is stronger.

It's a curious sensation...one I've never experienced before.

I don't like the thought of any harm coming to this little mortal—by me or anyone else.

When we arrive at her address, I frown as I take in the decrepit-looking old building. The interior is no better than the exterior, I note as I carry her up to her apartment.

Paint is curling and peeling back from the walls, and the smell of mixed cuisine wafting out into the hallways is more than a little nauseating.

I open her door with one hand while still cradling her close to my chest.

A quick survey of her tiny apartment has my frown deepening. The place is sparse, if neat and tidy.

I glance back down at the angel in my arms. *She deserves better than this...*

She deserves a castle. She deserves to be

draped in diamonds and silks and given all the riches and treasures her little heart desires.

My chest tightens again as I carry her to the bed and lay her gently down on it. My eyes rove over her as I take in her black skirt and button-up blouse with a frown.

If I want her to wake up and believe anything she remembers is just the result of a dream, then I don't need anything about her dress when she wakes up to be suspicious.

I'm not sure how she usually sleeps, but I'm pretty sure she doesn't sleep in her work clothes.

My eyes scan her room, and when I see a pair of pink pajama shorts and a tank top flung over a chair, I assume that's what she sleeps in.

I've undressed countless women over my lifetimes, but I've never felt such potent desire racing through my veins.

My hands are shaking as I slip her clothing from her body. My mouth goes dry when she's left in nothing but a simple white bra and panties.

She's a virgin. I can smell it on her like I can smell the blackest sin on others.

Maybe I should be a gentleman and turn my gaze away from her perfection, but I've never claimed to be a gentleman.

I allow my eyes to trace over every gentle dip and curve of her lithe body. I even go so far as to trace my fingers lightly over her shoulder, down her arm and over the gentle swell of her hip.

I grit my teeth and force myself to stop when I reach her panties.

I may be a monster, but there's one sin I've yet to commit, and I don't plan on starting now.

I refuse to take a woman without her permission.

Even some monsters have standards, it seems.

Her hair ripples as I lift her body just enough to slip her sleep clothing over her. As tempted as I am to remove her undergarments, I leave them on, afraid I would lose all semblance of control if I were to glimpse her naked breasts and that hidden treasure between her thighs.

As her hair moves, that flowery scent wafts up to my nostrils again.

My fangs descend again, and my vision sharpens as I breathe in deeply like a crackhead taking a hit from the crackpipe, seeking that one last high.

My arms tighten around her as I enjoy the weight of her in my arms.

If only...my mind begins, but I promptly shut those thoughts down.

There's no use pondering on what might have been.

I am what I am, and there's no changing that.

And this little angel doesn't deserve to be tethered to a monster.

She's innocence personified.

I force myself to release her, though I'm not sure how long I stand there just gazing down at her, watching the gentle rise and fall of her chest, the way she curls around a pillow like a sleepy kitten. My tortured soul is fraught with so many emotions—things I've long since thought myself incapable of feeling.

The first fingers of sunlight are filtering into the room when I finally tear myself away from her and go crawling back into my darkness.

Elena.

Keep reading Stalked by the Vampire here: https://books2read.com/stalkedbythevampire

SEX AND CANDY - EXCLUSIVE FREEBIE

She's too sweet to resist. And she's mine. All mine.

Ace

Three things are for sure:

One: She's the most stunning little thing I've ever laid eyes on.

Two: She doesn't belong on that stage, shaking it for men who don't deserve to breathe her air.

Three: She's already mine—even if she doesn't know it yet.

And I don't care what I have to do to prove it.

Candy

Only two things in life are for sure:

One: Nothing in life comes without a price.

Two: Men only ever want one thing.

But Ace? He's not like the others. He's dangerous, possessive, and makes promises I've never heard before. I should run... but every instinct in me tells me to stay.

Sex and Candy is a *steamy-as-sin* romance featuring an obsessive billionaire alpha who will do anything—*anything*—to claim his woman. He's intense, over-the-top, and completely irresistible. Protective? Yes. Possessive? Hell yes. HEA? Always.

Keep reading for a preview of Sex and Candy:

. . .

I take a sip of the subpar whiskey in front of me and grimace at the taste as I glance down at my Rolex. Fucker's late.

I drum my fingers on the table in irritation, keenly reminded of why I never let anyone pick meeting locations. You never know what kind of seedy joint they're going to want to meet up in or if they'll even show up at all.

I knew better than to let MacHay dictate the terms of this meeting, but I went against my better instincts and did it anyway. Simply because the man has proven so difficult to get in touch with. I'm regretting ever shaking his hand in the first place, and if I wasn't beholden to hold up my end of the bargain, I'd say fuck it and bail on this here and now.

Oh, well. You live and learn, right?

I'm tempted to do it anyway and am actually moving to slip out of my booth when the stage lights up and a hush falls over the audience.

I don't know what causes me to pause and sit back down. It's probably just going to be another subpar dancer like all the other ones that have been staggering around on the stage all night.

Maybe it's the pregnant pause of anticipation that seems to fall over the entire room.

I don't know.

But when the tiniest little angel I've ever seen steps on stage, time itself seems to stop.

Her skin glows ivory under the stage light. She has on a lacy white number, some sort of bustier, lacy panties, and white stockings. The look is topped off with fire engine red heels that match the paint on her lips. Long lashes frame light brown eyes that look too big and luminous for her little heart-shaped face. Long blonde hair like spun gold falls in glorious waves all the way down to an impossibly tiny waist that I know I could cup in my two hands. My breath catches in my throat. My god, she looks like a porcelain doll come to life.

But what most arrests me is the look in her eyes. For a split second when she first steps out on stage, her wide eyes are soulfully sad, so much so that they seem to take my breath away.

They seem to mirror all the tragedy in the world in their depths.

But then it's gone in the blink of an eye as she smiles, a dazzling, heart-wrenching smile that makes me instantly jealous. I'm irrationally upset that's she's gracing this roomful of men with that smile—that smile that I suddenly know deep down in my soul is meant to be only mine.

Mine.

Sultry music begins to play, and she begins to dance, gently swaying her hips as she flirts with the strip pole.

I'm gripping the edge of the table so tightly I'm surprised the wood doesn't break underneath my palms. I swear to God if one piece of clothing comes off her body I won't be able to stop myself from rushing up on that stage and covering her from prying eyes.

I'm aware that my reaction is insane. I don't know anything about this girl, but I can't stop the surge of possessive protectiveness that rages inside me at the thought of all these men seeing her so scantily clad like this.

What the fuck is she doing? Doesn't she know she's an angel? Doesn't she know she doesn't belong in here with all these devils?

I grit my teeth when she suddenly flings herself on the pole and begins to do a series of complicated flips and turns. The men roar and whistle and cheer, and I'd bet my last million half the fuckers in this place have a boner right now imagining her little body writhing on their laps like she is on that pole.

The thought fills me with murderous rage.

I'm so distracted by it that I don't even notice when MacHay finally takes his seat across from me until he chuckles and comments, "It's your first time witnessing the wonder that is Candy, huh?"

"What?" I bark at him, never tearing my eyes away from the beauty up on the stage. I feel like I won't be able to rest until her set is over and she's safely back behind that stage curtain where she belongs out of sight of lascivious male eyes.

He juts his chin out at the stage. "Candy. She's the feature dancer here." I spare a sideways glance at him out of the corner of my eye. He takes a sip of his drink and motions toward the stage with it, "And you can see why. Not only is she the prettiest one out of the bunch, but she's also the youngest and the one with the most skill. Consequently, she's the one Dan hoards to himself like the finest treasure. You can pay for a little extra with the other dancers, if you know what I mean, but Dan won't let anyone near Candy for no amount of money."

I frown, though I can't help feeling some sort of relief at the thought that Candy isn't being prostituted out. I can barely stomach the thought of all these men's eyes on her, much less their hands.

"So," MacHay rubs his hands together eagerly as Candy's show ends and she leaves the stage. I notice how she doesn't scramble to pick up any of the money thrown on the stage for her like all the dancers before her did. She walks coolly off the stage without even a backward glance at all the men she now holds in her thrall. "You really to get down to business?" MacHay interrupts my thoughts.

I scowl at him. The fucker keeps me waiting all the time, and then he shows up and expects me to cater to him. He can fucking wait now.

I level him with a cool stare before I stand from the booth and pull out my phone. "I have something to attend to first. If you want to see any part of this partnership go forward, you'll be sitting right here waiting for me when I get back."

He frowns and looks like he wants to say something, but one look at my tight jawline and he obviously thinks better of it, giving a curt nod of understanding instead. Yeah, he knows he fucked up.

I step out of earshot and call my head of security.

"Yeah, James? Get me everything you can on a dancer at the club on Sixth. Pronto. I want everything within the next thirty minutes. Goes by the name of Candy..."

Get your exclusive copy of Sex and Candy by signing up for my newsletter here: www.spicy-romance.com.

9 798215 735008